Lenny the Lazy Puppy

"Don't worry, Lauren," Lenny woofed. "I'm going to find your jacket."

Lauren bent down and ruffled Lenny's ear, but she and Michelle and Mr Miller were busy deciding where to search for the jacket. They didn't see Lenny sniffing the grass carefully, then hurrying away, his nose glued to the ground . . .

More of Jenny Dale's PUPPY TALES
stories follow soon

All of Jenny Dale's PUPPY TALES books can
be ordered at your local bookshop or are
available by post from Book Service by Post
(tel: 01624 675137)

Lenny the Lazy Puppy

by Jenny Dale

Illustrated by Frank Rodgers

A Working Partners Book

MACMILLAN CHILDREN'S BOOKS

Special thanks to Narinder Dhami

First published 1999 by Macmillan Children's Books
a division of Macmillan Publishers Limited
25 Eccleston Place, London SW1W 9NF
Basingstoke and Oxford
www.macmillan.co.uk

Associated companies throughout the world

Created by Working Partners Limited
London W12 7QY

ISBN 0 330 37362 5

135798642

A CIP catalogue record for this book is available from
the British Library.

Printed and bound in Great Britain by Mackays of Chatham plc, Kent

Chapter One

"Come on, Lenny! Fetch!"
shouted Lauren. "Fetch the ball!"
She threw the ball up into the sky
in a wide arc, and it bounced
down onto the grass.

Lenny, who was lying in the
sun, opened one eye and yawned.
Then he closed it again.

"I thought he was supposed to be a retriever," said Lauren's best friend, Michelle.

"He is," Lauren replied with a grin.

"Well, that means he's supposed to run after things and bring them back, doesn't it?" Michelle pointed out.

Only when I want to, Lenny thought lazily. He yawned again. It was quite a long walk from the Millers' house to the park and now they'd arrived, he wanted to have a snooze. He didn't want to run up and down after a silly old ball. Besides, he knew that Lauren would run after it and bring it back anyway, if he didn't.

"He's *supposed* to retrieve

things, but he doesn't," said Mr Miller, Lauren's father. They were strolling along a broad path between some beautiful rose bushes. "I don't think I've ever seen a lazier puppy!"

What a cheek! Lenny thought indignantly. *I'm not lazy. I'm just saving my energy.*

"Come and play piggy in the middle, Dad," Lauren called, running back with the ball in her hand.

"Er . . . no, thanks, love," said Mr Miller quickly. "I'll just sit on that bench over there and read my newspaper."

Lenny sat up when he heard that. "And he says *I'm* lazy!" he barked.

Lauren went over and stroked her puppy's shaggy golden coat. "Sure you don't want to play, Lenny?"

Lenny licked her hand. He loved Lauren, but he really didn't want to run around and get all hot and out of breath. He wanted to snooze in the warm sun.

Lauren and Michelle ran off

together across the park and began throwing the ball to each other. They were quite a long way away from Lenny but he could just about hear what they were saying.

"I had a great time at your birthday party yesterday," Michelle called to Lauren.

So did I, Lenny thought dreamily. He had lain under the table all afternoon, waiting for bits of birthday party food to be dropped near him.

"I loved the present you bought me," Lauren called back.

Lenny opened one eye and woofed his agreement. Michelle had given Lauren a pencil case with pictures of puppies just like Lenny all over it.

"Have you decided what you're going to buy with the birthday money your gran and auntie sent you?" Michelle asked.

Lauren shook her head. "Not yet."

Lenny stopped listening to the two girls and began to doze off. The sun felt deliciously warm on his furry coat and the long grass underneath him was soft and springy. He stretched out his shaggy paws and settled down even more comfortably.

"Dad!" Just as he was drifting off to sleep, Lenny heard Lauren calling her father. "Dad! We've lost the ball in the bushes and we can't find it!"

Mr Miller looked over the top of

his newspaper. "Have you had a *good* look?" he asked.

"Yes, we have," Lauren told him. "But we can't see it anywhere."

"We could get Lenny to help us look for it," Michelle suggested.

"We'll be here all day if we do that!" Mr Miller answered, smiling. He folded his newspaper and stood up. "Come on, I'll give you a hand."

Good, Lenny thought happily. *Now I can have a nice snooze in peace and quiet.*

A few seconds later he was fast asleep, dreaming of big juicy bones . . .

"Dad! Dad!"

Lenny woke up suddenly.

Lauren was calling again. He didn't know how long he'd been asleep but it could only have been a few minutes. He looked up to see Lauren and Michelle standing on the grass where they had been playing ball, looking very upset.

Lenny jumped to his feet and dashed over to the two girls. He couldn't bear it when Lauren was unhappy.

Mr Miller came out of the bushes. He had bits of leaves and twigs in his hair but he was clutching the ball triumphantly. "What's the matter, Lauren?"

"My – my jacket!" Lauren said tearfully. "I left it here on the grass while we were playing and now it's gone!"

"Oh, Lauren, what did you go and do a silly thing like that for?" Her father sighed and shook his head. "Someone must have taken it while we were looking for the ball."

Lenny whined and pawed at Lauren's leg. He wished now that he hadn't gone to sleep. Maybe then he would have seen what had happened to her jacket.

"What did you have in the pockets?" Mr Miller went on. "Anything important?"

Now Lauren began to cry. "My birthday money!" she sobbed. "All my birthday money was in it!"

"Oh, *Lauren!*" said her father again, looking cross. "You should have given it to me to look after."

"Never mind, Lauren," Michelle said. She put an arm round her friend's shoulder. "Come on, we'll have a look around and see if we can find it."

Lenny felt very bad indeed. If he'd stayed awake and guarded Lauren's jacket, then it wouldn't have been taken. He slumped at Lauren's feet. "It's all my fault," he snuffled to himself.

Then Lenny sat up again. "I have to try to put things right," he told himself sternly. He licked Lauren's knee. "Don't worry, Lauren," he woofed. "I'm going to find your jacket."

Lauren bent down and ruffled Lenny's ear, but she and Michelle and Mr Miller were busy deciding where to search for the jacket. They didn't see Lenny sniffing the grass carefully, then hurrying away, his nose glued to the ground.

Lenny wasn't worried about going off on his own. He knew how to find his way back home from the park if he had to. The most important thing now was to find Lauren's jacket – and get her

birthday money back.

He was a retriever, wasn't he?
Well, now he was going to
retrieve that missing jacket!

Chapter Two

At first Lenny was confused –
there were so many smells around.
But his sharp nose soon picked up
Lauren's scent. As he began to
follow the trail, Lenny detected the
scents of two other people as well.
*They must be the ones who took the
jacket*, he thought indignantly.

Sniffing this way and that, Lenny followed the trail off the grass and onto the path. He went along quite slowly. There were so many smells that it was sometimes hard to pick out the one he was looking for. He trotted further and further down the winding path.

"It's not here!" Lauren said, beginning to cry again. She, Michelle and Mr Miller had searched every centimetre of the grass where they had been playing, and they'd even looked in the bushes. But there was no sign of her jacket.

"Someone might have picked it up and taken it to the park

keeper's office," Michelle suggested.

Mr Miller nodded. "That's a good idea," he said. "I'm sure the park keeper looks after lost property. We'd better go and try there."

"Where's Lenny?" Lauren asked suddenly, looking round. "Lenny! Lenny! Come here, boy!"

But there was no sign of her retriever puppy.

"Oh no!" Lauren cried. "Now we've lost Lenny as well!"

"He's probably asleep somewhere," Mr Miller said crossly. "We'll just have to keep calling him until he wakes up."

"Maybe he's gone to look for your jacket!" Michelle suggested brightly. "He is a *retriever*, after all!"

Mr Miller shook his head and smiled. "I don't think so," he replied. "That puppy couldn't retrieve a bone if it was put right under his nose!" He picked up his newspaper from the bench. "Come on, you two. Let's go and find the park keeper – we can look for Lenny on the way."

Lenny was concentrating so hard that he didn't hear the footsteps behind him. Then someone spoke.

"I don't like stray dogs running round my park, Danny," said a stern voice. "If you find one, just call the Dogs' Home – they'll come and take it. Understand? There are far too many strays around here."

Lenny stopped in his tracks. He knew that voice! It was Mr Fraser, the park keeper. All the dogs who came to the park were scared of Mr Fraser. He was a tall, fierce-looking man with a little moustache, and he patrolled the park with an eagle eye. He didn't like litter, he didn't like noisy children and he didn't like dogs – especially stray dogs.

Lenny wasn't a stray, and he had a tag on his collar with his name and address on, but he didn't want to take any chances. He dived into a thick clump of bushes and ducked down out of sight.

Mr Fraser marched down the path, still talking. He was with someone Lenny hadn't seen before – a bored-looking young man with dark brown hair and glasses.

"There's a lot to learn about being an assistant park keeper, Danny," Mr Fraser was saying.

"This is only your first day on the job, so make sure you keep your eyes and ears open."

"Yeah, OK," said Danny with a yawn.

"Yes, *Mr Fraser*, if you don't mind," snapped Mr Fraser, frowning crossly.

Lenny waited until the two men had gone by. Then he tried to jump out of the bushes. But he couldn't move – his collar had caught on a large twig!

Lenny struggled and strained, frantically trying to free himself. But it was no use – he was well and truly stuck. There was only one thing left to do. Pulling backwards really hard, he squeezed his head out of the

collar, leaving it hanging on the bush.

He was free! But now that he didn't have a collar and tag on, he'd have to keep a sharp lookout for the two park keepers …

Lenny hurried over to the path again and sniffed around until he picked up the trail. After a few minutes it led him towards the large lake in the middle of the park. Then, suddenly, the trail stopped.

Lenny's heart sank. He ran round frantically in circles, trying to pick up the scent again, but it was no good. There were just too many mixed-up smells for him to find the one he was looking for.

He wandered along the water's edge, still sniffing the ground.

There were lots of ducks on the lake, as well as two swans, which bobbed up and down in the water, hunting for leftover bits of bread. Lenny kept a wary eye on them. He'd chased the swans once before when he'd come to the park. One of them had given him a nasty nip with its strong

beak. He'd never done it again!

Lenny stopped sniffing and began to feel miserable. It looked as if he would have to go back to Lauren without finding her jacket after all. Some retriever he had turned out to be. He hadn't found *anything*.

Lenny yawned and lay down under a tree. He was feeling a bit tired. All that running around had worn him out. Maybe he'd just have a little rest before he started looking again . . .

"Hey, you!" shouted a loud, familiar voice which made Lenny quiver all over with fear. "Get away from the water and stop chasing those ducks!"

It was Mr Fraser, the park keeper!

Chapter Three

Lenny jumped to his feet. Mr Fraser was racing towards him, his face red with anger. His assistant, Danny, was running along behind him.

Lenny couldn't risk getting caught, now that he didn't have his collar on! He turned and ran for his life. He raced away from the water's edge and back up the path. Mr Fraser and Danny were in hot pursuit.

"Come on, Danny, can't you run any faster?" grumbled Mr Fraser, as he lumbered along. "I want that dog caught – it's got no collar on – obviously a stray!"

"I'm – doing – my – best!" Danny wheezed, panting heavily.

"A young lad like you should be able to run faster than that!" Mr Fraser told him sternly. "*Aargh!* Get out of my way, you stupid creatures!"

The park keeper had to skid to a sudden halt as a crowd of ducks, and the two swans, waddled eagerly towards them, hoping to be fed.

Danny wasn't expecting Mr Fraser to stop quite so suddenly and he crashed into the back of the park keeper, almost sending Mr Fraser head first into the lake.

"Why don't you look where you're going?" roared Mr Fraser.

"It wasn't my fault!" Danny said indignantly. "You shouldn't have stopped like that!"

Mr Fraser glared at his new assistant. "I want that dog caught before it causes any damage in my park!" he bellowed. "Ow!" Mr Fraser jumped back as an angry swan nipped smartly at his ankle.

Lenny didn't stop running until he was a long way from the lake. Then he turned round and looked behind him. Mr Fraser and Danny were nowhere to be seen, thank goodness.

Lenny didn't know what to do. He was tired out and he'd lost the trail of Lauren's jacket. He'd never find it now.

He padded sadly down the path and back towards the place where Lauren and Michelle had been playing ball. He was looking forward to having his usual afternoon nap when they got home, but he really wished he'd been able to find Lauren's jacket.

While Lenny was busy running away from the park keepers, Lauren, Michelle and Mr Miller made their way to the office. It was a small, square wooden building which looked rather like a shed. It stood on the other side of the park, near the tennis courts.

"I hope someone's handed the jacket in," said Mr Miller as they walked along the path.

"So do I," Michelle added.

But Lauren wasn't listening. She

was looking around the park and frowning. "I'm more worried about Lenny," she said. "This is a big park – what if he really is lost?"

"Oh, I'm sure he's around here somewhere," Mr Miller replied as they stopped outside the office. "He's too lazy to go far. He'll come back if we shout loud enough."

"I don't think the park keeper's here," said Michelle.

Mr Miller knocked on the door, but no one answered. Then he tried the handle, but the door was locked. Mr Miller looked through the window. There was no sign of Lauren's jacket inside the small office.

"What are we going to do now?" Michelle asked, looking worried.

"I want to go and find Lenny," Lauren said firmly. "He might be getting scared all on his own."

Mr Miller smiled. "I expect he's asleep somewhere, safe and sound."

"I don't care," Lauren said stubbornly. "I don't care about

my jacket or my birthday money, as long as I get Lenny back!"

"Come on, then," said Mr Miller with a sigh. "We'd better go and look for him . . ."

Lenny arrived back at the place where Lauren's jacket had gone missing. He was feeling so tired he could hardly put one paw in front of the other. He couldn't wait to get home.

But there was no sign of Lauren, Michelle or Mr Miller. Lenny wondered where they were. He was sure Lauren wouldn't have gone home without him. They must be somewhere in the park.

He sniffed around until he picked up their trail and, nose to the ground again, he began to follow it.

The scent led him back to the path, then in the opposite direction, away from the lake. Lenny was glad. He didn't want to meet Mr Fraser and Danny again!

Lenny trotted on for a while, concentrating hard. But suddenly he picked up another scent. He stopped, feeling very excited. "That's the two people I followed before!" Lenny snuffled to himself. And the scent was getting stronger and stronger ...

Lenny raised his head and saw two boys coming down the path towards him. They were arguing at the tops of their voices and one of them was carrying something over his arm. Lenny recognised it straight away. It was Lauren's jacket!

Chapter Four

Lenny stared angrily at the two boys as they came nearer. Had they *stolen* Lauren's jacket?

Lenny began to growl softly, deep in his throat. If they had, they were in for a surprise!

"I thought you said you knew where the park keeper's office

was, Jamie!" the smallest of the two boys grumbled as they came nearer. "We've been walking around for ages now – Mum's going to be mad at us for being late!"

"Well, we can't just leave the jacket here, can we, Ben?" said Jamie. "Someone might be looking for it."

Lenny stopped growling. It sounded as if the two boys had found Lauren's jacket lying on the grass and decided to hand it in at the office. But they must have lost their way.

"Let's take it home with us," suggested Ben. "Mum will know what to do."

Lenny whimpered softly. If the

two boys took the jacket home with them, Lauren might *never* get it back! There was only one thing to do. He padded down the path to meet the two boys.

"Look, Jamie." Ben nudged his brother. "See that puppy?"

"He looks a bit young to be out on his own, doesn't he?" Jamie knelt down and held out his hand to Lenny. "Good boy! Come here!"

Lenny rushed over to him. But instead of letting Jamie stroke him he grabbed the sleeve of Lauren's jacket in his teeth and pulled hard.

"Hey, what are you doing?" Jamie laughed. He tried to tug the sleeve gently out of Lenny's mouth but the puppy wouldn't let go.

"Maybe he knows who it belongs

to," Ben suggested with a grin.

"Don't be daft!" Jamie tugged at the jacket again but Lenny clung on. "Come and help me get it off him."

Lenny began to feel nervous. He wasn't sure if he could hold on to the coat with both boys pulling at it. He did the only thing he could think of: he gave a fierce growl.

"Did you hear that?" Ben stopped and looked at Jamie. "He's dangerous!"

"He's just playing," Jamie replied, but he looked a bit scared himself.

"Well, his tail's not wagging!" Ben pointed out.

Lenny growled again, as fiercely as he could. This time Jamie dropped the jacket on the ground and backed away, closely followed by his brother.

"All right, all right, we're going!" he told Lenny. "You can *have* the jacket!"

The two boys ran off. Lenny barked happily. He'd done it! He'd got the jacket back. Now he was a real retriever!

Lenny was so proud of himself he felt he might burst! He couldn't wait to hear what Lauren, Michelle and Mr Miller would say – *especially* Mr Miller. They wouldn't be able to call him lazy any more!

Lenny pushed his nose into the pocket of the jacket. Lauren's purse was still inside, thank goodness! He tried to lift the jacket off the ground but it was too heavy.

He'd have to drag it along, he decided. The jacket would get a bit dirty, but Lenny didn't think Lauren would mind. After all, she was going to get her birthday money back – thanks to him!

Dragging the jacket was such hard work that Lenny didn't

notice two tall shadows creeping through the trees towards him. It was not until the very last moment that he saw one of the shadows coming up behind him. And by then it was too late . . .

A hand shot out and firmly grabbed the scruff of Lenny's neck. Lenny howled and tried to wriggle free, but he couldn't.

"Got him!"

"Well done, Danny!" said Mr Fraser, hurrying to join the assistant park keeper. "Now don't let go!"

"I won't," Danny said importantly. "What do we do now, Mr Fraser?"

The park keeper frowned at Lenny. "He's not wearing a collar

and identity tag, so he must be a stray. We'll have to send him to the Dogs' Home."

Lenny cowered behind Danny's legs, feeling very frightened. "I don't want to go to the Dogs' Home," he whimpered. "I've got a proper home – with Lauren!"

"Right!" said Mr Fraser. "Let's go back to the office and we'll phone the Dogs' Home and ask them to come and collect him."

Lenny began to shake with fear. Everything had gone wrong, and now he was in big trouble. If he was taken to the Dogs' Home, he might never see Lauren again!

Chapter Five

Lenny looked up at Danny and whined unhappily.

Danny took no notice. "I wonder where that came from?" he said, pointing at Lauren's jacket.

Mr Fraser picked it up. "Someone must have lost it," he

said. "We'll take it back to the office and it can go into the lost property box."

Lenny watched Mr Fraser reach over to pick up the jacket. The puppy had been *so close* to retrieving Lauren's birthday money – and now she would never know. It just wasn't fair! Lenny was so cross, he couldn't help giving a little growl.

Mr Fraser dropped the jacket and leapt backwards as if he'd been stung by a bee. "That dog growled at me!" he said, glaring at Lenny.

Danny shrugged. "I didn't hear anything."

Mr Fraser stared hard at Lenny and shook his head. "You can

pick the jacket up, Danny," he muttered.

"What?" Danny said. "I thought I was supposed to be holding the dog!"

"Well, you can pick the jacket up too, can't you?" Mr Fraser snapped.

Danny looked annoyed. "OK, you hold the dog and I'll get the jacket." Danny began to drag Lenny nearer the park keeper.

"Er . . . no!" cried Mr Fraser, backing away. "No, you keep hold of him," he said.

Lenny noticed that the park keeper didn't look at all scary now. In fact, he looked *scared*! In a flash, Lenny realised something very interesting . . .

Mr Fraser was frightened of him!

"Look, make your mind up, Mr Fraser," Danny said rudely. "Do you want me to get the jacket or do you want me to hold the dog?"

Before the park keeper could reply, Lenny tried another growl – a big, deep, fierce one this time.

Mr Fraser turned even paler, and this time Danny looked a bit nervous too.

"He's starting to get angry," Danny said, looking worried. "What shall I do?"

"You're not frightened of a young pup like that, are you?" said Mr Fraser in a shaky voice. The park keeper was pretending not to be scared, but Lenny knew better.

Lenny decided to help things along by growling loudly again and pretending to nip Danny's leg. Danny gave a howl of alarm and let go of Lenny.

Gleefully, Lenny rushed towards the terrified Mr Fraser.

"You idiot, Danny!" Mr Fraser roared. "He'll attack me now!" The park keeper tried to run, but tripped and fell over. "*Argh!*" he cried as the puppy bounded towards him.

At the last second, Lenny swerved past the quivering Mr Fraser and pounced on Lauren's jacket. He wasn't going to let them take it – and he wasn't going to let them send him to the Dogs' Home!

"Do something, Danny!" shouted Mr Fraser, who had now leapt up and taken cover behind a nearby tree.

Danny hesitated. Then he slipped off his coat and, holding it out in front of him, started to walk slowly towards Lenny. "Come on, boy," he said softly. "Good dog. Now keep still, you stupid mutt . . ."

Lenny growled indignantly, but Danny kept on coming towards him. Lenny knew that the man was going to grab him, but how could he run away? He had to stay and guard Lauren's jacket! Lenny braced himself . . .

Chapter Six

"What on earth's going on here?"

With a whimper of relief, Lenny recognised Mr Miller's deep voice.

Danny stopped in his tracks.

"Lenny!"

Lenny knew that voice, too. It was the one he loved most in the whole world – Lauren's!

He turned round and barked joyfully. There were Lauren and Mr Miller and Michelle. Thank goodness!

Lauren dashed down the path and scooped her puppy into her arms. Lenny wriggled happily, trying to lick Lauren's face while she kissed the top of his head.

Mr Miller looked at Danny, who was still holding his coat out ready to trap Lenny. Then he looked over at Mr Fraser, who was still behind the tree. "What's up? Is everything all right?" he asked.

Before anyone could answer, Lauren spotted her jacket lying on the ground. "There it is!" she gasped.

"So this jacket's yours then, Miss?" Danny asked her. Lauren nodded. "And the dog too?"

Lauren nodded again and hugged Lenny closer.

"We thought he was a stray," Mr Fraser said, coming out from behind the tree. "Why hasn't he got a collar on?"

"He *did* have one," Lauren replied, looking at Lenny's neck. "He must have lost it."

Lenny licked Lauren's chin to show he agreed.

"You see, I lost my jacket," Lauren explained. "And while we were looking for it, Lenny went missing too. Then I didn't care about the jacket – I just wanted my puppy back."

Lenny's heart swelled with love. Lauren cared about him as much as he cared about her.

"The pup had the jacket when we caught him," Mr Fraser explained. "We don't know where he got it from."

"Hang on a minute," said Mr Miller, looking surprised. "Are

you telling us that *Lenny* found this jacket?"

Mr Fraser and Danny looked at each other, then nodded.

"Lenny!" cried Lauren, delighted. "You clever boy! I *knew* you could do it!"

Lenny's tail wagged madly.

"You're a hero, Lenny!" said Michelle, scratching the puppy's ears.

Lenny woofed his thanks.

Mr Miller smiled. "I thought you were far too lazy to be a good retriever, Lenny. But I take it all back! Well done!"

Lenny barked and wagged his tail again. He could get used to all this praise!

"We were going to take the

jacket to our office, weren't we, Mr Fraser?" Danny said with a grin. "But the pup didn't want us to. And then when he started growling, Mr Fraser got scared—"

"That's enough, thank you, Danny," said Mr Fraser hurriedly.

"Oh, but Lenny's really friendly!" Lauren said, carrying the puppy up to the park keeper. "Look, you can stroke him if you like!"

Mr Fraser looked as if he'd rather pet a man-eating tiger, but he put out a cautious hand and touched the top of the puppy's head.

Lenny gave a little woof, and Mr Fraser jumped back, looking alarmed.

"He's just saying hello!" Lauren
grinned.

Mr Fraser smiled weakly and
gave Lenny another little pat.

Lenny wagged his tail madly.
He couldn't *wait* to tell the other
dogs he met in the park that
he'd just made friends with the
fearsome Mr Fraser!

"I think we'd better go home,"

Mr Miller said with a grin as Lenny yawned widely. "I think Lenny needs a nap – all that excitement must have tired him out!"

"It has!" Lenny woofed, yawning again.

"I'll carry you home, boy," said Lauren.

They said goodbye to Danny and Mr Fraser and set off for home.

Lenny snuggled down happily in Lauren's arms. He was going to enjoy coming to the park much more now that he wasn't scared of Mr Fraser.

"See, Dad?" said Lauren as they walked towards the park gates. "Lenny *did* find my jacket!"

"Yes, Lenny did very well," Mr Miller replied. "I thought he was too lazy to be a proper retriever, but he proved me wrong."

"Yes, I did," Lenny woofed proudly . . .

. . . and then he fell asleep.

Collect all of JENNY DALE'S PUPPY TALES!

The prices shown below are correct at the time of going to press. However, Macmillan Publishers reserve the right to show new retail prices on covers which may differ from those previously advertised.

JENNY DALE'S PUPPY TALES

1. Gus the Greedy Puppy	0 330 37359 5	£2.99
2. Lily the Lost Puppy	0 330 37360 9	£2.99
3. Spot the Sporty Puppy	0 330 37361 7	£2.99
4. Lenny the Lazy Puppy	0 330 37362 5	£2.99
5. Max the Mucky Puppy	0 330 37363 3	£2.99
6. Billy the Brave Puppy	0 330 39017 1	£2.99

MORE PUPPY TALES BOOKS FOLLOW SOON!

All Macmillan titles can be ordered at your local bookshop or are available by post from:

**Book Service by Post
PO Box 29, Douglas, Isle of Man IM99 1BQ**

Credit cards accepted. For details:
Telephone: 01624 675137
Fax: 01624 670923
E-mail: bookshop@enterprise.net

Free postage and packing in the UK.
Overseas customers: add £1 per book (paperback)
and £3 per book (hardback).